MW00908356

2007

Merry Christmas, Tessa!
   Love,
Papa Barry • Nana Heather
     Ox   Ox

For Sue – three cheers for chilly weather!

First published in Canada in 2007 by Fenn Publishing Company Ltd
34 Nixon Road, Bolton, Ontario, LZE 1W2, Canada.
Visit us on the World Wide Web at www.hbfenn.com

Copyright © 2007 Liane Payne

Devised and produced by The Templar Company plc,
Pippbrook Mill, London Road, Dorking, Surrey, RH4 1JE, UK

All rights reserved. No part of this publication may be reproduced, stored in a retrieval
system or transmitted in any form or by any means, electronic, mechanical, photocopying,
recording or otherwise, without the prior permission of the publisher.

Designed by Caroline Reeves
Edited by Sue Harris and Libby Hamilton

ISBN-10: 1-55168-317-2
ISBN-13: 978-1-55168-317-1

Printed in China

a goodnight story book

The Snowy Day

Liane Payne

Early in the morning, Bunny wakes up to find that something very exciting has happened. His garden has been transformed by a thick dusting of glittering snow! "Hooray!" says Bunny, rushing to put on his scarf. Just then, there's a knock on the door. It's Billy and Bella, Bunny's cousins. "Come out and play, Bunny!"

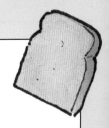

Billy really wants to go sledging, but Bunny doesn't have a sledge.

"Can we go skiing then?" asks Billy.

But Bunny doesn't have skis either.

"Well, I'm going to pretend-ski!" says Billy, using his long feet to slide along on the snow.

"I must give the birds their breakfast," says Bunny.

"Can I help?" asks Bella.

"I want to help too!" cries Billy, skiing over as fast as he can. But he knocks over the bird table, scattering food all over the lawn. "Sorry, Bunny," says Billy. "Don't worry," Bunny smiles. "I'll sort it out later. Today the birds can have breakfast on the lawn, while we decide what to do next. Up you get."

"Oh, please can we go skating?" asks Billy eagerly. But Bunny doesn't have any skates.

"I know!" he says. "Let's build a snowbunny!" Bunny and Bella start to pat the snow into shape. Billy thinks that building a snowbunny doesn't look like much fun.

"I'm going to pretend to skate!" he shouts and starts skidding up and down the icy path.

"Be careful, Billy!" calls Bella.

Before long, Bunny and Bella are putting the finishing touches to their snowbunny; a carrot for a nose and a warm scarf.

"Come and see, Billy!" calls Bella. Billy skates over to take a look, but he can't stop! He slides right into the snowbunny.

"Billy!" says Bella crossly. "You've ruined our snowbunny!"

"Never mind, Bella," says Bunny, helping Billy up.

"Why don't we have a snowball fight instead?" asks Bunny. Snowballs are soon flying in all directions. Most of them miss, landing in the snow. But Billy throws a large snowball at Bunny, hitting him right on the nose! "Bull's-eye!" laughs Billy, dashing away. "Billy!" says Bella, helping Bunny up. "That's not very nice!"

"Whee! Look at me!" calls Billy, skating past Bunny.

"Be careful, Billy!" says Bunny anxiously.

But Billy isn't listening. He's sliding faster and faster, until he reaches the end of the slippery path...

"Help!" cries Billy, landing with a CRASH on Bunny's favourite garden seat.

"Oops!" says Billy, looking sheepish.

"Oh dear!" says Bunny.

"Are you all right, Billy?"

The loud crash brings out Uncle Albert. "Now, what's happened here?" he asks. "Sorry about your seat, Bunny," says Billy. "I'm sure you didn't mean to break it," says Uncle Albert. "Bunny, help me to carry these bits over to my shed."

"All I wanted to do was have fun, but I've ruined everyone's day," sniffs Billy. Bella gives Billy a hug and says, "Why don't we sort some of these things out together?" First, Billy puts the bird table back up and Bella scatters breadcrumbs onto it. Next, Billy helps Bella to build a new snowbunny. He has to admit that they really are fun to make!

As Billy and Bella admire their snowbunny, Bunny and Uncle Albert appear, carrying something. It doesn't look like Bunny's seat. "We couldn't fix it," says Uncle Albert solemnly, "so I hope this will do instead…" "Wow! A sledge!" cries Billy. "Would you like to test it, Billy?" asks Bunny. "After all, you do like sliding about in the snow!"

Billy whoops with delight, whizzing along. "Wheeee!" he shouts. "This is much better than pretending to skate or ski!" The bunnies spend the rest of the day shooting along on the sledge, only stopping when Aunt May appears with steaming cups of carrot soup to warm them up.

"Thank you, Bunny!" says Billy. "This really has been the best snowy day ever!"

And later that evening, as Bunny snuggles up in bed, he thinks, "It truly was a wonderful snowy day. I hope the snow's still here tomorrow!"

Goodnight Bunny!